GIRLS ARE FANTASTIC!

A Collection of Short Stories for Girls about Strength, Love and Self-Awareness - Present for Girls

Amber A. Adams

ISBN - 9798849458779

This Book Belongs to

....

....

CONTENTS

LOTTIE'S LITTLE LLAMA

Lottie loved animals, but she lived in a small apartment in the city. Therefore, she was not allowed to have pets in her home. Luckily, when school was out, she could visit her grandparents' farm, where many animals lived. Her grandparents lived on a dairy farm with hundreds of cows, but they also had other animals, some to help with the work and some as pets. Lottie loved all the animals and looked forward to her summers playing with each and every one. She even helped her grandfather and some of the farmhands to milk cows very early in the mornings. Her favorite part was when the animals were new or just babies. At times, people called her grandparents when an animal was hurt or sick to see if they could nurse it back to health.

This year, Lottie would get to spend an extra month at her grandparents' house because the school schedule was changing, and she had more time off. She was already packed to leave the next day when her mother tucked her in tight for the night. That night, Lottie dreamed of all the animals, riding horses, milking cows, playing fetch with the dogs, and so much more. She was awake with the sun, but her mother made her eat breakfast before they could leave.

"Grandma always said that breakfast was our fuel for fun during the day," Lottie's mother reminded her.

"I know, I know," Lottie said in a huff.

Shortly after breakfast, they loaded up two suitcases in the car and headed to Lottie's grandparents' house. Lottie watched as the city buildings disappeared and the fields begin to appear. The city faded as the view turned into large fields, old barns, and different animals. Lottie looked out over the rows of wheat and corn, saw goats eating grass and a whole field full of fluffy black and white sheep. Finally, after a two-hour drive, they pulled onto the dusty gravel road that led to her summer home. The scent of cows, hay, and dirt was heavy in the air, but Lottie knew that meant a summer full of outdoor fun. She waited for the car to stop before jumping out and running toward the porch where her grandmother stood waiting.

Lottie's grandmother smiled as she hugged her granddaughter tight. Lottie could feel the lace from her grandmother's apron on her cheek and smell cookies baking in the kitchen. The car was unloaded, and Lottie's mother and grandmother went to enjoy some cold tea as Lottie went to explore the new animals that had come to live on the farm. She visited the cows first, knowing many of them by name. Next, she stopped in to say hello to Trigger and Ranger, the horses which helped move the cows between fields. Then, she found a stall with three little piglets sound asleep and a small pen where baby lambs and goats played together, jumping around like crazy. Lottie was excited to be able to play with each one and watch them grow all summer.

Back at the house, Lottie found her family members laughing and enjoying a sandwich and cookies. Lottie was happy to enjoy her snack and then ask her grandmother about all the new animals. The whole family gathered to talk and share, but most of the men had to get back to work milking cows and tending to the fields. The three women sat on the porch enjoying the warm sun and chatting about what was scheduled for the summer. Lottie's mother had to work, but she would visit on a few weekends. Lottie would spend most of her time on the farm and helping her grandparents. She wished all of them could live in the old farmhouse, but her mother's job was in the city. By late evening, her mother had to say goodbye. Lottie waved as she watched the car disappear down the driveway.

Lottie slept well that night, dreaming again of a summer filled with fun. She was up the next morning and surprised that everyone else had already been up for quite a while. Farm life started early. Grandmother had a big breakfast waiting and told her to eat fast that they had a call late in the night and had a new animal to go pick up. Lottie was excited, but her grandmother would not tell her what they were getting. She said it was a surprise and it would be Lottie's job to take care of this new animal all summer. It would need bottles to eat and lots of love. Lottie rushed through breakfast and got dressed.

When they got in the truck, Lottie saw several warm blankets ready for whatever baby animal would be riding back with them. She thought maybe a new goat or kitten or even a puppy needed help. They drove to a nearby farm as

Lottie dreamed of what was to come. When they arrived, her grandmother spoke to the farm owner, and soon a little creature was brought out wrapped in a fluffy blanket. Lottie could see a long neck and a puff of hair but did not recognize the animal. Finally, her grandmother took the bundle and uncovered the sleeping baby llama. Unfortunately, the mother had not made it, and the farm owner did not have time to offer the necessary care. Lottie grinned as she looked at the little alien creature that she instantly named Popcorn.

They climbed back into the truck, and Lottie held the llama on her lap. It woke up and looked at her with large, sad eyes but settled right back down into the blanket. The drive home was quick, and Lottie helped fix a stall for the llama. She added lots of sawdust, a little hay, and a warm blanket. Next, she made a bottle to try to get Popcorn to eat. The little creature did not know how to take the bottle, but he figured it out after trying for a few minutes. Popcorn would need bottles every three hours for a few weeks. This meant lots of nighttime feedings. Lottie sat in the stall with her new llama friend for hours that first day. She petted him, tried to get him to play, and fed him many times. That night, her grandmother fixed her a small area in the den to let Popcorn sleep inside and be fed every few hours.

Summer flew by. Lottie fed Popcorn each day, taught him to wear a halter and lead, and even taught him to fetch a small ball. The little llama was very attached to his new friend, even though he grew taller than her very quickly. Lottie's mother visited and met the new pet that would live on the farm forever. When summer ended, Lottie cried as she hugged her little llama, now very tall, goodbye. She hoped he would not forget her.

The following summer, Lottie visited again, and as soon as she got out of the car and called Popcorn's name, he came running. He was fluffy and fat, ready to greet his first friend. Her hard work had paid off, and she had a llama friend for life. How many other kids could say that they had saved a llama?

THE BIG CLEAN-UP

Brandy loved being outdoors. She enjoyed feeling the sun on her face, looking at all the plants, and seeing what little creatures may come out to play. Her favorite spot was a large creek that ran alongside a local park. Brandy had been going to that spot since she was little. Her father let her play in the creek, helping her catch frogs and lizards. Her mother taught her all the flower names and to identify the trees by the shape of the leaves. Brandy loved to go out to the park in her favorite outfit and play for hours. At ten years old, Brandy's mother trusted her to play with friends in the park, but she had to check in every hour by phone or by running home for a few minutes. Since her house was almost beside the park, this was easy to do.

It was finally warming up outside, and Brandy was excited to be able to play in the park every day. She asked her mom to stop by one afternoon after school to walk along the creek and explore the play equipment. Brandy noticed that over the cold months, it seemed like the park had been neglected. There was trash all over the ground and in the creek that Brandy had always loved. It was so bad that she did not want to play there. This bothered Brandy, and she was quiet on the short walk home.

"Mom, why is the park such a mess?" Brandy asked when they finally got home.

"Sweetie, some people do not think about how they hurt nature by leaving trash around," her mother answered.

"Can we do anything to help? I want to be able to play in a clean park again!"

Brandy's mom said they could make some calls to see if there were people to clean up the park, but she was not sure if anyone could help. They waited for a whole week, but no one seemed to know who was supposed to clean up the park. Brandy was worried that if the park was not cleaned, it would be closed down. She would not get to enjoy playing in the creek or swinging and running around with friends all summer. Brandy thought really hard about what could be done and suddenly had an idea. She could help clean up the park! Maybe some of her friends would help, they liked playing in the park as well.

The next day, Brandy asked her mother if she and her friends could work on cleaning up the park. Her mother told her she would be happy to get some trash bags and gloves, but the work would be on Brandy. Brandy agreed and started calling her friends to see if they could help. Three friends, Sean, Amy, and Sarah, agreed. They planned to meet early in the morning, the day after school let out for the summer. Two weeks later, they did just that. The four friends worked for two hours, picking up bottles, cans, and trash. They made sure to sort the items that could be recycled and put other things in trash bags they tied tight. They had made a dent in the mess but still had work to do. They met the next day to do the same thing and gathered four more giant bags of trash.

On the third day, Brandy and her friends met and were surprised to find three other children wanting to help. The group of now seven children only worked for an hour before it started to rain, but the park looked much better. A few days of rain kept the group away from the park, but Brandy was shocked to see several adults and children waiting when they returned the next Saturday. Word had spread that the beloved park needed to be cleaned, and this group of people was ready to help. It was a long day of hard work, but most of the trash had been picked up. A local businessman found Brandy and asked why she was working so hard. She told him she loved the park and nature. She wanted her park to be beautiful. He asked her if she would come back the following weekend with all her friends and helpers, he had a surprise planned.

Brandy ran home to tell her mother, who was very proud. She recognized the name of the businessman from the card he had left Brandy. A week later, Brandy walked to the park to meet

her friends and was surprised to see a long table full of food waiting. A group of men was waiting on the side, and all the people who had helped, clapped as she walked up to the gate. The businessman had planned a work party. The group cleaned up the rest of the trash, the construction men painted the old equipment, and a new swing set was installed. The park looked amazing. Before everyone left, Brandy was asked to stand in front of the crowd. She was thanked by the businessman and told that the park looked better than ever. She was presented with a gift basket full of fun summer toys for all her hard work. Brandy said thank you. She was proud to help, even when it was hard.

The park is still filled with fun and laughter every summer. Each year, on the day after school lets out, a group gathers to clean up and fix anything that needs repairing. It has become a yearly project that brings a smile to the faces of so many. It all started with one little girl trying to make a difference.

COOKING CLASS CHAOS

Savannah is a happy kid who is willing to do anything and be friends with anyone. She rarely gets upset or annoyed. While Savannah loves to color with her sister and play with blocks with her baby brother, she most enjoys baking. She likes to bake cookies with her mother and then spend time decorating them carefully with icing. At only eight years old, she is already pretty good at decorating and getting better at baking. The only time Savannah ever got really upset and angry was when her baking did not go as planned. She wanted her desserts to be perfect and taste the best every time.

One afternoon, Savannah's mother and father asked her to come to talk to them. She did not know what was happening but walked into the room and sat down on her favorite chair. Her parents were smiling as they handed her a brochure. She looked at the picture on the front, a bunch of kids smiling, cooking in a big kitchen. Savannah read the title "Cooking Class" but was still confused.

"Honey, we signed you up for cooking classes so you can learn to bake and cook new foods," Savannah's mom finally explained.

Savannah stared speechlessly. She could only utter the word, "Really?" Finally, the news sunk in, and Savannah could do nothing but smile. She would attend two classes a week and learn new skills each week. Her parents explained that by the end, she would be able to make a whole meal. They knew she liked to cook, but this would help her get even better. She was almost too excited to sleep that night. Savannah dreamed of freshly baked pies, her favorite spaghetti, and even fixing dinner for her whole family. Still, she worried she might not be good at everything that needed cooking.

The next day, right after school, Savannah was dropped off at her cooking class. She walked into a giant room full of stoves, ovens, and big mixers. Each station had an apron lying on the counter and a stool to stand on so the children could see over the counter safely. She watched as seven more children filed into the room. Two were the same age as Savannah, but the rest were older and taller. Savannah took a spot up front and tried on her apron, ready for the first lesson. The teacher walked in with a big smile. She was a short, blonde-haired woman in a bright blue apron that looked like it had seen years in the kitchen. The teacher spent 30 minutes explaining how the class would work and what types of food they would cook. Savannah was excited to hear they would learn to make meatballs, apple pie, and even easy homemade ice cream.

The first lesson was making different types of eggs. This was an easy breakfast that every kid should know how to make perfectly. The class was taught how to break an egg open and scramble them quickly. The teacher also taught them to make an omelet with ham and cheese, one of Savannah's favorites. Then it came time to make fried eggs. The teacher talked about how important it was not to break the yolk, or it was not a fried egg. Savannah tapped her first egg on the side of the counter and was shocked when the yoke broke as it slid into the pan. She took a deep breath and tried again. It took three more tries before she could crack an egg and not break the yoke. Finally, the egg was cooked well, and it came time to flip it over to cook on the other side. Just as she put the egg back in the pan, the yoke broke. Savannah was ready to scream. It seemed like everyone else had already cooked their eggs.

The teacher walked over to help. She explained that the great part about cooking was that sometimes the mistakes could lead to something amazing. She encouraged Savannah to try again but to stay calm as she broke the shell. It was not about being perfect. It was about creating something to feed our bodies. Savannah had never thought about cooking in that way. She wanted everything to look good and taste okay but had never thought about why we needed to cook food. She gently tapped the eggshell, and it slid out perfectly. When it came time to flip the egg, she took a deep breath and gently flipped it over. It looked beautiful.

Classes continued for several weeks, and Savannah learned to make many new dishes. The last evening, the families were invited to watch their young cooks and enjoy the meal they prepared. Savannah was excited as she started her special dish. She was going to cook macaroni and cheese with ham pieces and make a salad. She started with her salad, and just as she finished, the bowl fell to the floor, spilling everywhere. Savannah looked shocked but simply cleaned up the mess and started again. Then, she started on her macaroni, carefully cooking the pasta, slicing up the ham, and layering in the cheese sauce. She had help moving the big dish into the oven and had to wait as the cheese melted and the dish finished. Savannah sat with her family as she waited. Suddenly, smoke poured out of the oven, and her teacher ran over to see what happened. The cheese had bubbled out and burned, making some of the pasta hard and small burned areas to appear.

Savannah sat down and cried as she looked at her far from perfect meal. Then something amazing happened. Her family came over, hugged her, and took the dish to the table. They ate around the burned parts and enjoyed a big salad together. Finally, Savannah understood what her teacher meant. The food was fuel for fun and family. Something that could be shared. The cook may not have been without mistakes, but having a good time together was better than any dish she could cook.

GIRLS RACE TOO

The flyer read "Pinewood Car Derby" with a picture of a small pinewood car at the bottom. The race was free to enter for all children ages 5- 13. All it took was a homemade pinewood racer and an entry form signed by your parents. Cate loved the idea of building a pinewood car. She had seen the kits in the toy store many times. She also knew she loved to build about anything. Her father was an architect, and while she could not build a whole building in real life, she was already practicing with her Legos. So, Cate grabbed the flyer and ran home to show her father.

Cate's father was excited to help his only daughter build a pinewood car, but he told her she would have to do the work. He would help when she needed it, but she would have to read all the directions and build the car. This included painting it when she was finished. He knew how fun it could be to created something on your own.

He also knew his daughter was smart enough to build the car from the kit they would buy. That evening, Cate and her father went to the toy store to look for a pinewood car kit. Cate knew exactly where they were. She had looked at them before. She grabbed the box and went to find some paints for the car to be decorated. She chose her favorite colors of blue and purple. As Cate and her father walked to the counter to pay, she noticed a couple of boys from her school.

"Are you making a pinewood car for the derby too?" Cate asked.

"Yeah, all the BOYS are entering the derby," they said to make a point.

"I can enter too," Cate said with confidence.

"Yeah, right! No girl is going to win a race against us. Girls should not even be allowed to enter."

Cate walked away, looking for her dad. She was close to tears. When she found him, he asked what was bothering her. "Dad, are girls allowed to build pinewood cars?" She asked.

"Of course! Girls can do anything they set their minds to, even build pinewood cars!"

Cate still wasn't sure, but she still wanted the car kit. She could decide later if she was going to enter the race. Cate worked for two weeks to get the car just right. She spent three more days painting the car bright blue with tiny little flowers across the top. Finally, two days before the race, Cate's dad asked if she was getting excited. Cate stared at the floor, still thinking about the boys who said girls could not race.

"Cate, honey. what's wrong?" Her father asked.

"Girls are not supposed to race," she answered.

"Who told you that nonsense? Whoever it was does not know how well a girl can race, or they are scared they will lose." He said, grinning.

"Okay, Daddy. I'll try," Cate half-smiled.

On the way to the race that weekend, Cate still was not sure she should compete. However, when they parked the car, she was excited to see several friends, boys and girls, holding their own pinewood cars. Cate jumped out of her seat, eager to show off her creation. Her father helped her sign in, and they waited for her race. She would race against two girls and three boys, all from her school. Two of the racers were the boys she had seen in the store. Even before the race, they laughed at the girls trying to race against boys.

When the bell rang for their race, Cate and the others set their cars on the track. The bar dropped, and all the cars raced down the steep incline. Cate watched as her car became a blue blur flying down the track. Finally, the cars reached the bottom, and Cate won second place. Another girl in her class had taken first. They all smiled and congratulated each other. The two boys from the store came in last. They came over to say they were sorry and congratulate the girls.

"I guess pinewood car racing is not just for boys," one said.

"We are sorry that we were so rude. Your car is great," said the other.

Cate smiled. She may not have won, but she was brave and took part in the race. She was proud of building the car, painting it, and not being afraid of others making fun of her. She could not wait until the race next year.

THE UNIQUE PUPPY

Kiya was so excited that her parents had finally agreed to let her get a puppy. She had been asking for three whole years, but now that she was turning ten, they finally agreed it would make a wonderful birthday present. Kiya had often thought about what type of puppy she wanted, but she liked them all. Her parents told her they would go to the animal shelter to look around and see which ones she liked best. Kiya was so excited she could barely wait for the weekend when they would go.

When the weekend rolled around, she was up early, ready to choose her new best friend. Her mother had to remind her that the shelter did not open for a few hours, so she needed to wait. Kiya was so excited she could barely hold still, but she managed to hold things together until it was time to go. They pulled up to a long, grey building with big glass doors. Kiya could hear dogs barking and kittens meowing. She wished she could bring them all to their house, but her parents had only agreed to a puppy. They went inside and asked to see the dogs.

Kiya walked down rows and rows of cages filled with barking dogs. Some were big and fluffy, some tiny and squeaky. Some dogs were brown, others black, a few were all different colors. Kiya checked out each cage slowly as her parents stood back, willing to let her make the decision. At the end of a row was a large cage with an empty child's swimming pool filled with blankets. Inside the pool were six little puppies that were all resting in a pile. Two were solid black, one was solid white, and the other three were white with black patches. Kiya sat down in front of the cage to watch the puppies sleep.

As each puppy woke up and started moving around, Kiya saw the seventh puppy. It was smaller than the rest and had a bandage around its stomach and a spot where one leg was missing. It had one ear that stood straight up, and the other flopped to the side. Kiya knew the puppy was different, but she was already in love.

She called her parents over to see the little ball of fluff with only three legs and big dark eyes.

"Oh, Kiya, don't you want a puppy that can run and play like other dogs?" Her father asked.

"What about one of the other puppies in the litter? They all look cute and playful." Her mother encouraged.

Kiya had made up her mind, she wanted the little puppy with three legs, and she wanted to know his story. So Kiya and her parents went to ask about the puppy. The shelter worker explained that the puppies had been found alone in a box, but the little one with a missing leg had a serious injury. He had surgery right away to remove the leg and was healing well, but he still seemed sad. That was enough for Kiya. She knew she could help the little puppy and wanted to take him home. The shelter said they could have him, but he had to stay for two more weeks until he could heal.

"Can I visit him?" Kiya asked with a hopeful smile.

"Of course! I think he could use a friend." The shelter worker was glad the injured little puppy would have a good home.

Every day the shelter was opened, Kiya would visit the puppy for an hour. Sometimes she would sit and hold him, telling him how brave he was and how they would play when he was completely better. Sometimes, she would read him a story from a favorite book. Other days, she would try to get the puppy to play, but he still seemed scared. He could walk but preferred to lay down or cuddle up on Kiya's lap. Kiya did not mind. She loved the puppy she had named Firefly. When Firefly was healed, Kiya was ready to bring him home. She had a bed in her room, a new collar and leash, and a few small toys for playtime.

Two weeks after she first saw Firefly, Kiya's parents took her to the shelter one last time. She would get to bring him home, and he would be hers forever. When she walked to his cage, he hopped toward her, knowing her voice. The little puppy seemed to know he was going home. The worker opened the cage, and the puppy hobbled right up to Kiya to be picked up. She scooped him up and told him it was time to go home. Firefly licked her face and nuzzled into her arm. Within minutes they were in the car headed home. Kiya never minded that Firefly was different because it made him special. The two already shared a bond. Firefly never left Kiya's side when she was home. Kiya knew she made the right choice. Being different made Firefly unique, and Kiya felt it was an honor to be his owner.

TAKING FLIGHT

Sasha loved to travel, and at age 10, she had already visited several states in the United States. Every summer, her family would pack up the minivan and visit someplace new. The family had visited the mountains where they camped and then swam in lakes and rivers, once playing in a real waterfall. Sasha's mother suggested a trip to the ocean one year, and they stayed in a small rental home on the beach. Sasha loved running barefoot in the warm sand and watching dolphins jump out of the water in the early mornings. So far, Sasha's favorite trip had been to New York, where they spent an entire day walking around Times Square, taking in all the sights.

This year, the family would make a very special trip to visit Sasha's grandparents in Italy. The trip would not be in the old beat-up van but on an airplane. Sasha had seen airplanes take off and land many times but had never ridden in one. She was nervous about the trip but wanted to visit her grandparents. To prepare for the trip, the family had to get their picture taken for passports because they were leaving the country and then pack enough clothes for an entire week. The passports took almost 6 weeks to arrive, but Sasha was super excited to see her picture in the little book.

Two weeks after the passport came in the mail, the family loaded into the van and drove to the airport. Sasha was surprised at how big the airport was and how many people were walking around, moving in all directions. Sasha and her parents carried their suitcases to a big open area that formed a long line. Sasha's mother had her pack a separate bookbag with a few small toys, some crayons, a book, and some pages to color and draw on while on the plane. As they waited in line, Sasha watched the huge airplanes land and take off. She started to get a little scared, knowing they would be so high up in the air for so long. The flight was over 8 hours long.

After a long wait, Sasha and her family had to wait some more in long rows of chairs with other people waiting on their flight. When their seats were called, Sasha gathered her bookbag and held her mother's hand as they boarded the plane. The seats were very close together, and Sasha got to sit by the window. She realized how high up the plane was, even before taking off. Sasha was feeling nervous as the airplane roared to life. She could feel it picking up speed as they moved down the runway. She held her mother's hand as the airplane lifted off the ground, and they moved into the clouds. Sasha held her mother's hand for an entire hour before she could relax.

As Sasha relaxed, she started to look out the window at the clouds. They were so close it felt like she could touch them if the windows could be opened. When the flight attendant came around and asked if anyone wanted a drink or a snack, Sasha enjoyed a cookie and a small soda. Sasha relaxed enough to color and draw as they soared through the air. As she watched the sunset from the plane window, she wondered why she had been so scared to fly. Many hours later, the airplane landed in Italy. Sasha was so excited to see her grandparents waiting to pick them up. Italy was amazing.

"Mom, can we go on airplane trips more often?" Sasha asked, ready to travel everywhere in the world.

"We can plan a trip every few years." Her mother answered with a grin. Flying is a little more expensive than driving.

Sasha could not wait to start planning. She wanted to fill her passport with stamps from different countries. She was so glad she was brave enough to enjoy the airplane flight and had the chance to see her family. The flight home was much easier for Sasha; she was not nervous. She knew that the first time trying something new was always the scariest, but she could be brave when needed.

THE SOLO

Jasmine was only nine, but she loved to sing. Her mother used to tell her she was born a singer. Before she could say a word, she would make sounds to any music played in the house. When Jasmine was only three, she would sing her dolls to sleep every night. At five, she sang with the children's choir at church. Now, at nine, Jasmine had been asked to sing a solo for the school talent show. Jasmine knew she could sing, but in front of the whole school and parents seemed scary. She told her mom that the music teacher asked her to sing. Her mother told her it was her choice, but she had a beautiful voice that needed to be heard.

Jasmine had three days to let the music teacher know if she would sing. She wanted to because she loved to sing and make music. However, she was scared to sing because of how many people would be there watching. She had sung in church, but it was a small group, and she knew everyone. The school would mean lots of parents, all the kids, and teachers. She worried she might mess up or forget the words to whatever song she chose. For two days and nights, Jasmine tried to decide if she would sing. Finally, she decided to be brave and sing in the talent show.

The talent show was a whole month away, so Jasmine spent every afternoon practicing her song. Her mother said she even sang in her sleep some nights. Jasmine knew if she wanted to do well, she had to put in the work. Her mother was very proud she was willing to sacrifice her time and energy to do her best. She told Jasmine that winning the talent show was never as important as doing the best she could. Jasmine knew this lesson well. She liked to win at things but knew it took time and practice. Even with all the time and practice, she knew she could not win at everything, but she could be proud of the work.

The night of the talent show arrived, and Jasmine put on her new, sparkly dress. She felt like a queen in the shimmering dress that reflected the light. Her mother put her hair in braids and even let her wear lip gloss. Jasmine felt the butterflies in her stomach as she climbed into the car.

"Mom, I am not sure I can sing in front of all those people," Jasmine whispered.

"Sweetie, if you get scared, remember that you have practiced hard. Just close your eyes and sing from your heart. That is where the music starts," Jasmine's mom reminded her.

Jasmine took a deep breath and relaxed a little. They pulled into the school parking lot, and Jasmine looked at all the cars. There would be lots of people in the bleachers tonight. Before Jasmine's mom turned off the car, she looked at Jasmine. She reminded her that it was about having fun and sharing what she had practiced for so long. She reminded Jasmine to close her eyes and sing from the heart. It would be perfect. They walked in together, just as the show was about to start. Jasmine would be the closing act, so she had almost an hour to wait before her turn. The whole time, she could hear her mother's words in her head.

Finally, it was Jasmine's turn to perform. She took one last deep breath and walked on stage. Her music teacher started the music, and Jasmine stared at the crowd. Then, she saw her mother, who smiled and gave the thumbs-up sign. Jasmine smiled back, closed her eyes, and sang from her heart. Her voice filled the whole room. When the music stopped, Jasmine opened her eyes and listened to the crowd clap. Her butterflies were gone. She had faced her fear and sang from the heart. She walked off stage, beaming. Best of all, after the show, lots of people came up and told her how good she had sounded. They were surprised at her voice and happy she sang for the whole school. Jasmine knew she would never be afraid to sing again because she had put in the work and done her best.

THE HAUNTED HOUSE

Talia loved autumn because the leaves on the trees changed colors, and the air had a slight chill. Talia also liked all the traditions her family had in the fall. She helped her grandmother can fruits and vegetables and got to pick out new, colorful sweaters to wear to school. Best of all was when October started, and all the Halloween traditions began. The whole family went to a pumpkin farm and picked out pumpkins to carve. While at the farm, they walked through the corn maze and drank warm apple cider. Some years, there was a hayride with lots of friends and a campfire that followed. This was definitely Talia's favorite time of the year. The best part this year was Talia turning ten. At ten, Talia was old enough to go to the town's haunted house.

Talia had three older brothers who went to the haunted house every year. They seemed to love it. She had always wanted to go but was too young. Now, she was finally old enough and looking forward to the family event. The haunted house would open in two weeks, and Talia was already too excited to stay calm. Talia's parents were not sure she would like the haunted house, but she really wanted to go. The day after they told her she could, Talia was so excited to go to school and tell her friends.

Talia sat on the school bus the next morning, waiting for her best friend to get on so she could share her news. When her best friend took her seat, Talia started talking right away.

"I am so excited I get to go to the haunted house this year!" Talia squealed happily.

"Aren't you afraid of all the scary things?" Her friend asked.

"What scary things? Isn't a haunted house just silly and fun?" Talia asked.

"My sister went last year and said she was so scared she cried," her friend answered.

Talia just stayed quiet. Maybe she was not old enough to go to the haunted house. She was afraid she would cry and be called a baby. She did not want to face scary things. Talia's good mood was gone, and now she was just worried. She thought about that haunted house all day, forgetting how excited she had been the night before. That afternoon, after school, Talia stayed in her room thinking about the haunted house. She asked her brothers what it was like when they walked through. In normal big brother style, they told her it was so much fun and so scary that they never knew what would happen. Talia smiled, but inside she felt fear rising up.

"Mom, I am not sure I want to go to the haunted house," Talia said as she watched her mother prepare dinner.

"You were so excited. What happened?" Her mother asked.

"What if I get scared and cry, or a monster gets me?" Talia asked quietly.

"Oh sweetie, you know the scary things in the haunted house are not real, right?"

"But my friend said her sister cried and that she saw monsters and witches," Talia answered.

"Talia, sweetie, Halloween and haunted houses are meant for fun. The people that work in the haunted house are wearing costumes. While it can be scary at times, it is not real, and no one will get hurt."

Talia sighed in relief but still was not sure she wanted to go. Her mother told her it was her choice, but she hoped Talia would face her fear. Talia thought about the haunted house every day. She wondered if she was brave enough to go. Finally, the day came to go, and Talia had to decide whether she wanted to or not. Talia decided to go, even though she was scared.

The family pulled up to the big, dark building. A tape of scary noises played loudly over the speakers. Talia's mom reminded her it was just a tape, but Talia was ready. She knew she could face this building and whatever was inside. She walked by the building often, and it was not scary. At the door was a big sign that said "Beware," but Talia was brave enough to look past it. The big metal doors creaked open, and the dark hallway looked weird with flashing lights and noises from every side. Talia held onto her mother's hand as they walked slowly down the hall. Suddenly, a giant fake spider fell from the ceiling, and Talia screamed. It surprised her, but when she realized it was not real, she laughed. Around a corner, a scarecrow reached out to grab those who walked by, but Talia noticed he did not move very far. This haunted house really was fun.

It took 45 minutes to walk through the whole building that ended with a maze of mirrors to find the door. Talia had a wonderful time. She had faced her fears and enjoyed the event. There were scary parts, but Talia reminded herself it was fun, not real. Talia felt proud of facing her fears, even if it was hard. She knew she could face anything if she tried.

A SPECIAL BOND

Abby was five when her mother told her she would have a baby brother or baby sister. Abby had been excited and thought the new baby would come from the store. She wanted to pick out a sister. So, when her mother explained that a new baby would come from Mommy's tummy and take several months before it arrived, Abby was surprised. The first few months, no one said much about the baby, but soon, her mother started getting a little belly. Abby's mom told her it was because the baby was growing.

A couple more months passed, and Abby's mother got even bigger. She said the baby was growing, and soon they would find out whether it was a boy or girl. When Abby's mother went to the doctor to find out whether it was a boy or girl, Abby was allowed to go. The doctor put some kind of slime on her mother's tummy and waved a magic wand over it. A picture appeared on the screen, and the doctor seemed to know that the baby was a little boy. Abby was a little disappointed because she did not even see a baby, just a moving blob. Her mother told her the baby still had to grow and would soon look more like a baby. On the way home, Abby's mother told her they needed to come up with a name, and now that they knew it was a boy, they could start shopping as well. Abby loved to shop, so she was excited.

When they got home, Abby's mother told her that a baby needed all kinds of things and asked if she would help her pick out a new crib, some toys, and some clothes. Abby agreed right away. Then, when her father got home, they started talking about names.

"Can we name him Dolphin? It is my favorite animal." Abby asked.

"I think we need a different name, maybe not an animal." Her mother chimed in.

"How about macaroni?" Abby said, knowing she loved macaroni and would love her brother.

"That may not work either, but those are good options." Her mother said.

Abby's mother told her they would not decide that night but wanted Abby's help choosing a name. Abby went to bed, still trying to help find a name. A week later, as they were sitting down to dinner, Abby's mother told her they had four different names and wanted Abby to pick one. She was going to name her new baby brother. Abby was so excited. She had to choose between the names Spencer, Jaxson, Hunter, and Alex. Abby knew right away which name she liked. She stood up, walked over to her mother, and talked to her belly.

"Hi, Jaxson. I am your big sister Abby. I cannot wait to see you." Abby said with a smile.

Abby's mother and father smiled, happy with her choice. Abby's mom said she thought the baby liked the name because he moved when Abby introduced herself. Abby got up again and put her hand on her mother's belly, talking softly to the baby inside. She felt a ripple, and her mom told her it was her brother moving. Every night after, Abby talked to the baby. She read him books and sang her favorite songs.

A few months later, Jaxson was born and came home. Abby got to pick out his first outfit for the ride home. She was so proud of her new brother, even if he did not do much yet. Abby told him stories every day. She helped feed him a bottle sometimes too. The only part she did not like was when he cried. Abby did not want to see her little brother sad and crying. Her mom told her that babies could not talk, so sometimes they cry to get what they want. It was still hard to listen to his cries.

Late one night, a storm woke baby Jaxson up. It was loud, windy, and thunder shook the house. Jaxson screamed for over an hour. Even though Abby's mother and father had tried walking him and rocking him, Jaxson was still scared and crying. Abby used to be scared of storms, too, so she understood. That is when she had an idea. She walked into Jaxson's room and sat beside him in his swing that gently rocked back and forth. His little face was red and wet from screaming and crying. Abby told him a story as she held his hand and then sang her favorite song. Jaxson got quiet, watching his big sister sing. Then, slowly, his eyes closed, and he fell asleep. Abby's mom knew there was a special bond between the brother and sister. That night, Abby slept in her sleeping bag beside Jaxson's crib, and he only woke up to eat, not because of the storm. Even a whole year later, Abby's singing can calm Jaxson down in a few minutes. She is an amazing big sister.

THE BIG DONATION

Evie loved animals, especially dogs, but their apartment was not big enough to have a pet. Thankfully, Evie's mom loved animals too, and she let Evie be around animals as often as she could. Each weekend, they volunteered at the animal shelter. They cleaned cages, bathed animals, and even walked the dogs. Sometimes, Evie was allowed to play with the puppies to get them used to being around people. She loved the time they spent there, even though it was hard work.

One weekend, Evie heard the shelter workers talking about all the puppies and kittens they had to take care of each day. They were worried that there was not enough money to feed all the animals and definitely not enough to get them blankets and toys. While food and shelter were important, something to play with and cuddle up in was also needed. Evie listened to them talk and had a great idea. She could help.

Something that few people knew about Evie was that she loved sewing, arts, and crafts. Her grandmother had taught her to sew when she was only five, and she had just gotten better as she grew. At the age of nine, Evie could sew pretty well. She knew she had lots of material at home and could sew blankets for all the little animals. At least they could be warm in their cages until they found new homes. Evie told her mother what she wanted to do. Evie's mother had an even better idea. They could send a message to their friends to get their extra material too. That way, they could make even more blankets for all the animals.

When the pair got home, Evie's mother sent a Facebook message to several friends telling them what they were doing and asking for material. Every day the next week, people dropped off material, or a package arrived full of supplies. Soon, the dining room table was covered in material, thread, and even a few toys that friends had sent to donate. Then, Evie and her mom got to work. They spent every evening sewing small blankets to give all the animals a nice place to cuddle together. At the end of the month, they had 20 blankets done. Word had spread fast, and more people continued sending fabric and asking if they could send food and toys for the animals if they did not have fabric.

At the end of the month, Evie and her mother loaded up all the blankets, toys, and donated food. The whole car was filled with just enough room to sit down and drive. They pulled into the shelter and were surprised to see all the workers standing out front. They had kept the project a secret, but the secret was out. All the workers clapped as Evie, and her mother started unloading the car. Everyone was so happy to know the animals would be comfortable and well-fed with all the donations. Then something even more amazing happened. Evie walked through the doors to see a giant pile of toys and even more food sitting in a large open room. It turns out when people heard about Evie's project, they had sent even more donations to the shelter in her name. The shelter had enough treats, food, and toys to last for months.

Evie smiled so big that all her teeth showed. She was so excited that the animals could be happy and well cared for at the shelter. She had not meant to do something so great; she just wanted the animals to be happy. Now, they would be so much happier, and no one had to worry. Since fabric was still coming in each day,

Evie and her mother kept making blankets. So far, they have made over 100 blankets, and the animals are often sent home with one to help them adjust to their new family. Evie is truly amazing.

FINALLY HOME

Joy had lived in four different houses in her first nine years, but she only remembered the last two. Now they were moving again because of her father's job. While Joy did not like changing schools so often, she had learned to make friends easily and now knew people worldwide. Joy was lucky enough to have lived in Spain for almost a year, in Italy for a few months, and now they would be back in the United States for a while. She was very good at helping her mother pack up their home and knew how to label boxes that went into her room. She was very careful to pack her art supplies because they were so important to her. She loved to draw, paint, and color as often as possible. Joy's father promised he would try to make this their last move, so Joy was really excited.

Joy had only gotten to see pictures of the new house. It was big and white with a bedroom that her mother said could be decorated any way she wanted. The house had just been built, so they would have to shop for some furniture and big items, like a refrigerator. As they drove for hours in the car, Joy started drawing pictures of what she wanted her room to look like in the house. She was tired of her pink room and wanted something bright. She knew she was getting a new bed because she had gotten so tall her feet hung off her old one. They would stay in the house tonight and start shopping tomorrow. Tonight, they would carry in boxes and camp indoors in the living room. This was a tradition in every new house.

After the longest car ride ever, Joy looked up to see their new house. It was big, two-story, and white. Joy jumped out of the car and waited at the door while her parents looked for the key. When the door was opened, she ran from room to room, checking it out.

"Your room is upstairs on the right," her mom yelled from another room.

Joy ran upstairs and opened the door to a big, bright white room that was much larger than the apartment they had lived in last. She had a closet to herself, a place for her bed, room for an art space, and so much more. Joy ran to the window and looked outside to see the best surprise ever. She had a yard to play in that was surrounded by a big wooden fence. A tall oak tree grew in one corner, and the grass looked like the perfect place to run and play. Joy ran back downstairs to help her parents unload the few bags and boxes they had. She hoped this would be their forever home.

"So, what do you think?" Joy's mom asked.

"I love it! There is a yard and everything," she squealed.

"Well, we have a surprised for you, but it will not be delivered until tomorrow afternoon," her mom answered. "Later, we will go shopping for some furniture for your room if you like."

Joy was ready to get new stuff. She felt like this could be their last move and wanted to make a room of her own that would last. After unpacking the few things that moved with them, Joy and her mom went shopping. They spent hours picking out beds, kitchen appliances, and even a new couch. They would be getting deliveries for the next two weeks as the house filled up. Joy's favorite shopping was picking out a new paint color for her room. She chose a light purple with neon-colored flower stickers to add more color. Her mom was excited to help decorate. After a long day, they went home to rest. The family ate pizza on the floor of the living room and fell asleep on air mattresses.

The next morning, the doorbell rang early. The deliveries were already beginning. First to come was the refrigerator and stove. Joy watched as they cut open the boxes that were bigger than her and put everything in place. Next came her bed, dresser, and a small desk her mom had picked out. These were set up in her room which would be painted later. That afternoon, the doorbell rang again, and Joy's father said it was her surprise, but she could not see it until it was ready. He told her to stay inside while everything was being put together, then headed into the yard.

Joy had to wait four whole hours before her father came back inside to tell her the surprise was ready. Joy had to close her eyes and be led outside. When she opened them, she saw the most amazing little house she could imagine. There was a sign on the door that said "Joy's Art Studio." She screamed and ran to the door to look inside. It had two small rooms, a wall-sized chalkboard with lots of colored chalk, a table filled with crayons and coloring books, and an easel with all new paints. Joy ran back out to give her father the biggest hug ever.

"Did you see the message on the chalkboard?" He asked with a grin.

"What message?" Joy asked as she ran back in to see what was written.

The message she found made her cry. It read, "We are finally home! No more moving. We love you." Joy could not believe it. She ran back out to hug both her parents as they all cried and smiled. The word home had never meant so much.

NATALIE LEVELS UP

Natalie had always been an active little girl. Her mother used to say she ran before she could walk. Natalie had been known to climb twenty feet up into a tree before most people could get off the ground. She was always easy to find, with her bright red curly hair bouncing in the breeze and her shining green eyes peeking out between the branches. Still, Natalie liked anything that kept her moving.

When Natalie was only four, her mother thought it would be good to enroll her in some classes to use up this energy. First, she tried to dance, but Natalie did not like dancing. Next, she tried gymnastics, which was okay, but Natalie got bored. It was not until Natalie was put into a karate class that she really had a good time. In karate, she was active, listened well, and yelled some as part of the class. Natalie was really good at karate. She was always one of the best students, and by the age of six, she was outperforming most of the others who were a few years older.

Each time you learned and mastered new skills in karate, you had to show them in front of a group and, if good enough, got another belt. If you were under eight, the belts were usually all white with different colored ribbons attached. When you moved into the older class, the belts were a solid color, with the highest rank being a black belt. When Natalie was old enough, she was moved to the youth class. Before she could attend classes, she had to earn the lowest belt for that age, a white belt. This was easy for Natalie, who had been in karate class for years.

On the first day of the new class, Natalie was excited. She walked into class, ready to show off. She took her place up front but moved further back when other people in the class showed up. She was surprised to see all the other kids who were taller and already had purple, green, and even red belts. She was the shortest and youngest in the whole class. Natalie took part in class but stayed toward the back. A larger student called her shrimp and laughed at how little she was, but she focused on the instructor.

That evening when Natalie's mother asked her about class, Natalie cried. She was so upset that she was so much smaller and scared she would not be the best ever again. Natalie's mom explained to her that you never start on the top.

You have to work hard, practice, and keep getting better. It was not going to be easy, but if Natalie really wanted to get better, she had to keep working at it. Natalie said she was not sure, but she would think about it before the next class.

"Sweetie, I hope you continue to do karate. You are good at it, and you have always had fun," her mother said as she was tucking Natalie into bed. Natalie gave a half-smile and snuggled down into her blankets.

The next week, Natalie was busy with school and homework. She had not decided whether she wanted to go back to class but had to decide by the next morning. She decided to try. Natalie worked hard and got better, but her first chance to move up to a gold belt was only a week away. She knew she could do it, so she was willing to try.

When the day came for the test and hopefully a new belt, Natalie did her best but failed. Some of the other kids laughed and made fun of her. She was ready to give up. Natalie's mom reminded her that everyone had to practice and she would have another chance soon. Natalie wanted to quit but also wanted to keep learning. She made up her mind to keep trying. Every day for a whole month, Natalie practiced her moves and skills. She spent at least an hour a day practicing. When it was time for the next test, she knew she was ready. Natalie was the last person to take her test. She was shaking as she stood in front of the class and guests. This time, Natalie nailed every skill with ease. The instructor handed over her gold belt with a smile and a bow. Natalie's mom hugged her tight and then helped her switch belts. Natalie was so proud of herself for sticking with it. Even the kids that had made fun of her told her how well she had done. Natalie is still doing karate, but now she has moved up to a green belt. Whether she is the best or not, she is a champion for trying.

DISCLAIMER

This book contains opinions and ideas of the author and is meant to teach the reader informative and helpful knowledge while due care should be taken by the user in the application of the information provided. The instructions and strategies are possibly not right for every reader and there is no guarantee that they work for everyone. Using this book and implementing the information/recipes therein contained is explicitly your own responsibility and risk. This work with all its contents, does not guarantee correctness, completion, quality or correctness of the provided information. Misinformation or misprints cannot be completely eliminated.

Made in the USA
Las Vegas, NV
14 January 2023

65590435R00049